BILLY GOATS GRUFF

BILLY GOATS GRUFF

THE ORIGIN

ROAR MIKALSEN

Life Liberty Books

To Liv and Anton

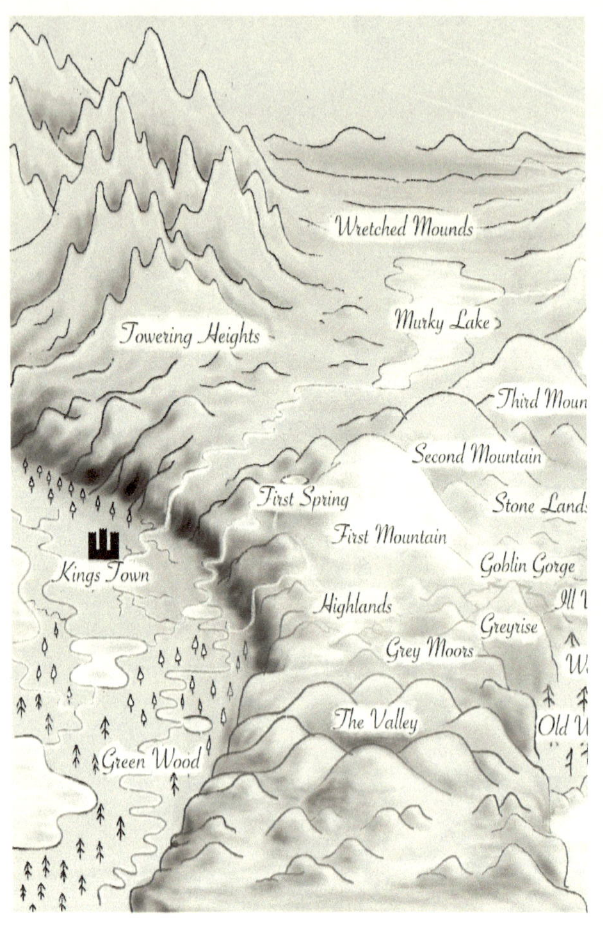

Worldmap (Northwest)

Worldmap (Northeast)

CONTENTS

~ 1 ~

TRIBE AND SETER

Once upon a time, there were three billy goats called the Gruff brothers. They were hungry after a long winter and wanted to go to the Seter[1] to eat themselves fat.

The Seter was far away, past several mountains. The mountains were not the worst. Worse still was a bridge that they had to cross because under it lived a troll.

The youngest goat, merely two summers old, had never been there before. The middle one, seven summers, had not been there either. But both had heard their big brother talk about the troll under the bridge. Old Hermit, the oldest goat on the grassy slopes, used to narrate a story of how there was a heath with grass so full of delights that the goats in the old days were willing to defy seven mountains to get there. Even so, one day, a troll appeared, and it had been troubling them ever since.

The troll liked to eat animals and travellers inevitably fought for their lives. The goats in the small valley, therefore, had given up the trek to the Seter long ago. They still talked about the good old days, but these days had been replaced by the trials of everyday life, and so the years passed—very many years.

Thus, the dream of the good life at the Seter had become a memory, something the young goats—and a few older ones—talked about. These were considered the rebels of the pack by those who were sceptical about the existence of such a place. In fact, quite a few did not even believe in the troll because, as the years went by, the desire for adventure also disappeared. The goats adapted quickly to their diminishing horizon and the common assumption arose that this was probably how things have always been. Yet, they did not journey into the mountains. The fear of the unknown was simply too great, and most animals preferred not to think about it. The Gruff family were no different. Neither Grandfather nor Grandmother, Mom nor Dad cared for what happened outside the valley. But the three brothers were different. They had grown up listening to Old Hermit's legends, and the big brother increasingly felt the urge to get to the bottom of this.

To him, the mystic stories put everyday life in a poor light. Even the colours had lost their appeal, and he was disillusioned with the habitual pecking order. There was not much sun or greenery in the valley and what little there was had been taken by others. The water was not good either. The big brother had noticed it for a while, but no one wanted to hear it. They were more concerned about fighting for territories while he thought it would be better to fight the troll.

Not that he was afraid of the other bucks. He had not yet lost a fight, and he felt confident that it would always be so. Nonetheless, he realised that the old ways were no longer for him, and thus, he had been planning this journey for a year.

He had also spoken with his brothers. They were both convinced that their big brother was the coolest kid in the vale. They also agreed that life in the valley was not the best. Its shadows seemed to grow darker, the grass harder to find, and the water worse. Hence, they were enthusiastic when one summer day, their big brother, asked if they were ready for an adventure.

Big Billy Goat Gruff had also spurred others. He had told them about the possibilities on the other side of the mountain. He had spoken about problems with the old and proffered solutions, but the rest of the kit were not convinced. They were not sure if the troll needed to be battled or even confronted. Nor were they confident that it was better elsewhere, or as convinced as the brothers about their big brother's excellence. They chose instead to stay.

The three brothers therefore said their goodbyes to the herd.

They hugged their friends, one by one, and set out on a voyage. They crossed the Gray Moors and the Highlands and encountered no troubles in the climb over First Mountain. The weather was good and even the eternal snow seemed easy to conquer. Second Mountain was just as trouble-free, though the youngest had become tired. They had been moving for a long time and they needed rest.

The three bucks therefore found a place and settled down. "How are you?" the big brother asked.

Little Billy Goat Gruff replied, "I have seen more than most goats have seen in a lifetime, but no troll. Do you think it is a long way?"

Big Billy Goat Gruff responded, "It's hard to say. But if Old Hermit was right, we must cross a waterfall on the other side of Fifth Mountain. There is only one road across Rouge River, a bridge, and that's where the troll lives."

The middle brother broke in, "But maybe we can find another way? Maybe we could go in that direction?" he asked, looking south.

"No," said the big brother. "That's where the Misty Mountains are, and no one finds their way through them. Far more goats have disappeared in the fog than those who have faced the troll."

"In fact, I have yet to hear of anyone who has returned. We should continue on this path."

After a short rest, Little Billy Goat Gruff got up. The big brother sharpened his horns. He was eager to reach the bridge, and the brothers joined.

They kept on their journey. Summer faded and autumn approached before the goats came to Fifth mountain. They rounded its peaks and, after a while, saw the bridge.

The smallest was shaking. It was one thing to hear his big brother's fairy tales, but it was another to be close to origins of myths. He wanted to turn around. "I'm scared," he said. "I don't even have horns. What can I do?"

The middle brother was also anxious. He longed for home. The big brother felt it, too, but did not show it. He remembered what the sage had told him and knew better.

"Fear is a liar," Big Billy Goat Gruff replied. "Old Hermit said it was okay to be afraid, but one should not listen to their fears."

The brothers were not reassured.

"You and your old goat!" the second brother countered. "You know neither Mom nor Dad cared much for his stories. They thought he was a dreamer and that he should relate to things as they are rather than how they should be."

Middle Billy Goat Gruff remembered how father and mother had laughed at the mystic. "That old goat has a loose screw," their parents always said. Like the rest of the tribe, they did not appreciate ideas that were beyond the ordinary—and the old goat had made it his mission to think along those lines.

The second billy goat continued: "Do you remember how he upset Mommy when Grandfather became ill?"

The hermit had told mother that life was a gift from the gods, that there was a reason for everything, and that death was natural. This had become too much for their mother. She loved Grandfather far too much to find solace in such ideas and drove the eremite out of the house when he added that the fear of death was as silly as the fear of life and that it was important to see beyond it.

The middle brother thought of their valley. It was perhaps mostly just rock and sand, and the water was probably not the best, but it appeared much more tempting than an encounter with the troll.

"Isn't it better to turn around?" he persisted. "We could bring more friends and come back another day."

The youngest listened. He, too, had heard others laugh at the hermit, but Big Billy Goat Gruff said, "The herd is a terrified lot. Since the troll appeared, their world has become smaller and smaller. They no longer dare to climb the mountains, and even at home they sleep poorly. Perhaps the recluse said some strange things. But he created, with his thoughts, his own reality and grew older than anyone."

Big Billy Goat Gruff continued, "Whose example will you follow? The hermit talked of cosmic consciousness. Of a universe that is alive, that thinks itself into reality, that operates according to certain laws, and that is on our side. He said that fear and love rule everything and that we have been given free will to create the world that we want. I do not know much more about this than you. But I do know that I would rather live for a dream than go back to a tribe that gave up long ago."

The big brother shook his head. "You both know that if we turn around, it's the end of the adventure. You have seen the fear of the herd. No one wanted to come with us. The mere idea of a troll makes them weak, and if we do not dare, our dream is dead. I therefore suggest that we use our guile. We do not even know if the troll is there."

The youngest was more hopeful now. The idea of another winter in the vale was not enticing. "Perhaps we can tiptoe?" he said meekly. "If the troll really is there, maybe he wouldn't notice us if we're quiet?"

The middle brother had also regained his courage. The idea of slipping past the troll was not impossible and he suggested that the little one should go first. Since the kid treaded so lightly, if anyone could get past the bridge unheard, it was him.

The little brother saw his point. He was still scared, but he had confidence in his big brother and that there could be a happy ending even if the troll showed up. They thus came up with a plan before Little Billy Goat Gruff headed for the bridge.

It was quiet. The wind had almost subsided and only a murder of crows could be heard down in the gorge. Heroically, the little billy goat walked towards the crossing. He looked around but there was no one to be seen. He tried a few steps.

Trip-trap, trip-trap, went the bridge.

It was still quiet. He took a few more steps, before he suddenly heard something moving.

"Who is that tripping over my bridge?" rumbled a deep voice from the depths.

"Oh, it's just me, the youngest Billy Goat Gruff. I'm going to the Seter to make myself fat," he replied in his sweetest voice.

But it did not help. The troll was not charmed and shouted back, "Now I'm coming to gobble you up!"

The youngest billy goat could feel the ground moving. Some crows flew up. He almost jumped but kept his composure. "Oh no!" he yelped. "Please don't take me for I am too small. Just wait till the second Billy Goat Gruff comes. He's much bigger."

He heard grumbling. Serious dismay arose from the depths below the bridge, and it was not quiet till the troll shouted, "Well, off with you!"

Some time passed and then came the second billy goat. He had seen how his little brother had made it across, and he walked towards the bridge.

Trip-trap, trip-trap, trip-trap.

Immediately, he heard the voice from the depths, much closer this time:

"Who is tripping on my bridge?" growled the troll.

"Oh, it's just me, the second Billy Goat Gruff. I'm going to the Seter to make myself fat," he replied. His voice was not as sweet.

"Now I'm coming to eat you alive," roared the troll.

"Oh, no! Don't take me," said the middle buck. "Wait a bit longer till Big Billy Goat Gruff comes. He's much larger. He's worth the wait."

"Very well! Then go," said the troll.

More time passed. And then came Big Billy Goat Gruff.

Trip-trap, trip-trap, trip-trap.

The buck was so massive that the bridge creaked and groaned.

"Who is that tramping over my bridge?" he heard from the depths.

"It is I, Big Billy Goat Gruff!" said the goat, his voice almost as rough as the troll's.

"Now I'm coming to gobble you up," roared the troll.

"Well, come on!" thundered the big brother. "I have horns as big as spears. With them, I will take your eyes! I have the strength to break boulders. With it, I will crush both your body and bones!"

Suddenly, a hand emerged from under the bridge. It tried to grab the goat, but he leapt away again and again. The rest of the troll was on its way up. He yelled and rattled the bridge, but the big billy goat was ready. He mustered all his courage, charged, and sprang at the troll—right in his face! Now the troll screamed even more, but the big buck was ready. Once again, he charged at and gored the troll, who lost his footing and fell down the cascade.

What a fight! The brothers, who had been watching it all, came running. They were overjoyed! They bounced all over the place. "Big brother," they squealed, "you did what no one could, you beat the troll! No one has fought like you!"

The big billy goat strode towards the others. "Yes," he said. "This is a great day. Now the path to the Seter is clear. It has not been so for hundreds of years. But that is how it is. And perhaps it is true, as the old sage said, that a bit of courage is all it takes to change the world."

"I know one thing: as the troll came over the edge, the Capricorn of Light was on my side. I felt a strength I have never known. Time expanded and everything slowed down. Still, it was as if we were fighting for an eternity. I realised that the troll was a part of me and that a greater force connects us all. Now I'm a little confused."

The second billy goat looked at him and laughed. "You hit pretty hard. In fact, I have never seen such a leap. Are you sure your head did not crack?"

"I felt this power more strongly than anything else," replied Big Billy Goat Gruff. "The Capricorn, the troll, we, and everything around us are one. I know that now. But it is still strange how the troll fits in."

The little brother then came over: "I

think the cascade got rid of him. I don't think we need to worry about that anymore. But the fact that you took him out, big brother, that's incredible! Everyone is going to be really proud of you now!"

The biggest billy goat was pleased. "We'll see," he replied. "There are more mountains ahead. A lot can happen. There are probably more trolls in the world. But now I believe that they can not only be conquered but also be tamed."

He looked at the others. "There is a lot between heaven and earth. But there is more between light and dark and the game that follows. Even Old Hermit did not know that we were going to stand here victorious. And it is a consolation that the worst is now behind us."

The second billy goat looked towards the peaks ahead. The terrain was unknown, but the road went on. "I have no idea what we have in store," he said. "But far away, do you see it brightening?"

The others saw it too. Far, far away, the light really had a different colour. There, past Last Mountain was Goldcrest, the legend of ancient lore, and in that direction, the three brothers journeyed.

They walked and walked. The closer they got, the more the sky opened, and after a journey they would not forget, they finally arrived.

There was the Seter! The grass was not only golden, but there were fruit, berries, and flowers they had never seen before. It was as if everything sparkled, and the more they ate, the more their fear and melancholy washed away. With every bite and chew, the world appeared more beautiful. Out there on the field, as they ate and frolicked, also the others got to know the energy that had taken over their big brother at the bridge. With it, the gears of the cosmos aligned, and synchronized with the essence of their being. The world was turned inside out and time appeared to stand still, but to their surprise everything fell into place. The oneness of everything became apparent and a holy spirit emerged in all. Its wisdom and kindness was infinite. Its presence absolute.

This is how the brothers spent their days. They grazed away. It was as if summer would never end. The cosmos was in complete harmony, and the three billy goats enjoyed life on that heavenly heath.

THE LOST CHAPTER

The three Billy Goats Gruff had been on the Seter for a long time. They had grazed and grazed and had never felt so good and full, but something was missing. The tribe was still in the valley and the little brother kept thinking about Mother.

"This outdoes everything," he said to his big brother, "but I miss Mommy and our friends. Now that we are here, shall we not return to show them the way?"

The big brother nodded. He had been

waiting for this. "Life has never been so good, but others are struggling," he replied. There is room for everyone. Of course, we must go back. Have you talked to our brother?"

Second Billy Goat Gruff was laying in the grass, dreaming. But this time, something was different. Rather than pleasant dreams of flight and light and idyllic visions, he was in a desolate, snow-covered landscape and everything was bleak. He did not know who he was or where he was. All he had were his footprints. They walked backwards in the snow and he followed them.

He walked like this for a long time with nothing but the trail. The atmosphere was heavy and sorrow covered the land like a thick blanket. He walked and walked. Things did not get better. Instead, he came to a familiar place. He could not place where he had seen it before. Everything was hidden by a veil.

There was only snow and footprints. But the more he traced them, the more he realised that he had crossed this path before. In fact, it dawned on him that he was going in a circle and that he was in the power of a secret being—something that was hidden and could not stand the light. He felt like a pawn in a great game and like he could not free himself from the magician's control.

He did not know how he woke up or came to his senses, but suddenly, his little brother was there.

"Are you ready?" he asked.

Second Billy Goat Gruff rose to his legs and looked around. He understood what he was talking about and that they had to go. But this dream was strange, and so he told the others about it.

Big brother looked at him with concern. "Something is wrong," he said. "This place is nice. But the dream would not have come if it were complete. I take it we have been here too long. I fear the herd is in danger. Let's go."

The three goats gathered all the grass they could carry and set out on the journey home. They walked and walked. As they followed the road back to the bridge, they were happy to discover that the troll was still gone.

The youngest brother nodded contentedly. "Well, that's that!" he said. "That troll must have learned his lesson. I believe the rest of the way will be easy."

The middle brother nodded too. "Yes," he said. "Now there's just the wolves and the snow. It went well when the weather was good, but things are not as before. I have no idea how long we've been gone, but the weather is colder and the landscape heavy with sorrow. It might have just been a dream, but I'm worried."

They had all sensed this. The further they travelled from the Seter, the more it seemed like a memory, and gradually, the three goats sensed danger lurking. Their instincts were right. They had not journeyed for long when a snow leopard at the top of Last Mountain reminded them of their stark reality. The mother had to feed her kittens and Little Billy Goat Gruff almost had his leg torn off when she dug her teeth into him. It did not look good. Even so, the speed down the rocks was too much and the leopard had to let go to avoid the rapids when the goat tumbled down the incline.

Fortunately, he was able to drift off to safety and was greeted by his brothers on the other side. They still had the hay from the heath. The grass had begun to turn brown and taste dry. Even so, it helped the little kid get back on his feet, and after a few days, they were on their way.

With this episode in mind, they knew that

the wolves could be their end. They enjoyed the fresh air and the freedom of the road, but an old, primal fear was back. All the way, the goats were on guard. They no longer felt safe, and the oldest brother stayed awake while the others slept.

This is how the journey proceeded. The happiness that they had felt on the heavenly heath faded like the grass, but they did not see wolves. Instead, a mysterious creature appeared on Third Mountain. It was a stoat, which was natural seeing that they inhabit this mountain, but this one was not as shy as others. He looked like one who had always wandered and always felt at home, and the three billy goats were impressed by the little fellow who came their way without fear.

"Who are you?" asked Big Billy Goat Gruff.

At a distance, they noticed an arctic fox on the prowl. It looked hungry, and with one eye on the creature, they listened to the stoat's reply.

"If you are anyone, you are everyone. You should know that better than most." He laughed a joyful, trilling laughter. The fox was getting closer, but he remained untouched. The tiniest billy goat said: "You see that fox? He looks hungry. Why don't you hide among those rocks?"

The stoat looked at the youngest and said, "I see that you've been hurt and that you've been through great danger. But we are all here despite danger, visible and unseen."

He looked at the others and continued, "Like you, I have been through more than it seems. I have also met the Capricorn. I too have encountered the nastiness of trolls, but in the appearance of a charming ferret. I know that the unseen dangers should be feared more. And I have yet to meet a fox worse than her."

He laughed again. "We are sustained by a force, a pulse, which has a bigger picture in mind than you and I who are just trying to get through each day. We animals eat each other, as it has always been. But a time will come when we shall live side by side. You are part of this plan, and that is why we are all here, including the fox."

"I know she can hear me. I know she has her own problems. She herself is afraid of the eagle, which soars up there, and she has lost several litters to the snow. It just spreads. As winter gets tougher, summer gets shorter and we are all under this strain. We thus have an interest in finding a solution."

The fox could not understand how the stoat knew her so well. But she took a liking to the little guy. She looked up and spotted an eagle high up there circling for prey.

"I hear you," she said.

"The mountain life is getting harder and harder. There are hardly any eggs to be found, and my cubs are starving. But so are others. There are rumours of a curse. The crows are everywhere. They bring bad news, and many are getting sick. I don't know what to do."

The eagle circled closer. The stoat was still calm, and the fox would not be worse. She resisted the urge to hide and tried instead to appear untouched by matters of life and death.

The eagle swooped down for a landing. It aimed at a murder of crows, which made a racket before it disappeared. The eagle moved closer and began to speak.

"I hear you too, rascal, and I have news. A cabin has been found on First Mountain in the eternal snow. Around it, the crows gather, but not even our seers have observed who lives there. All they know is that he does not come from this side. He changes shape and is surrounded by a darkness. Our seers therefore call it Murk Mountain."

Big Billy Goat Gruff looked at the eagle. He had many questions, but the stoat spoke first.

"The darkness has been gathering for a long time. Only now do we begin to see what we are dealing with."

He studied the eagle. "We ermines know that your seers are not the most observant, and we have long known that the earth is deteriorating. Even the plants have gathered as much. They know there is a poison in their roots. They know that it comes from the water of a wizard on First Mountain. The First Spring is not well. The fact that the eagles have gotten wind of the obvious merely indicates a shift. It means that we have reached the end of a cycle and that we have a job to do."

He looked at the others. "These are the times of which the Prophet foretold. Long ago, the Wisest had a vision where he saw the Ages as chapters in a great book. He saw time as a river that paved way for greater creation, a force whose purpose was to fully know itself, and that we were all part of this river. He said not only are we part of it but that an era would come when we would see the world with new eyes and understand that we are all this great river—in its entirety."

"Ever since, our oracles have been watching the stars. They have seen smaller cycles come and go but believe that a greater upheaval is near."

Middle Billy Goat Gruff looked at him. "You would have liked Old Hermit," he said. "You would have had much to talk about."

"But the world is only getting darker. What if we talk to our friends and they talk to theirs? Could we tell them about a place, just five mountains away? There, there is a meadow like none other. One where the world is no longer terrible. One where everything is fresh and there is room for all. We can go there to recuperate. We can also discuss tactics and what should be done with Murk Mountain."

The youngest billy goat nodded. He missed his family and looked forward to seeing his friends. It would be quite an exodus, he imagined, when they together defied the darkness and headed for the Seter.

"Let's go," he said. "I cannot wait to tell Mother what happened. Let's now travel back and gather those we can. We'll tell them about the darkness, about the wizard who destroys the water, and then go back to the heavenly heath."

Everyone agreed, except the stoat. He believed the solution was closer. He thought of the trolls and wanted to talk to them. But where were they?

The three brothers had not seen anyone on their way back. The stoat therefore wanted to head north, towards the Wretched Mounds and the Towering Heights. The eagle mentioned the possibility of finding trolls in that direction.

Even so, the journey was long and the goats were not ready for a diversion. They wanted to go home and warn the valley. As a result, the stoat flew with the eagle north. The fox went to alert the wolves, while the three brothers continued on their journey home.

They were heartened by the meeting with new friends and after a few days, they saw the snow on Murk Mountain. There was obviously something amiss. The water was worse, but the goats had to drink, and they felt the unrest rising.

Up there was another enemy, maybe worse than the troll. Who was he? Why did he poison the water? Not even the big brother had any idea what to do. But they had to get to the valley. The climate, which had been good on the trek to the Seter, was now cold and unfavourable, and they were trying to move unseen.

Still, they felt as if someone was constantly watching them. The atmosphere was thick and more and more crows were flying over them towards the snowy peaks.

They decided to head towards Grayrise and cross Goblin Gorge, a ravine that ran like a wound in the landscape. It was a rocky and difficult area in the south. However, it was easy to find shelter there, and on the other side were forests. The three bucks hoped that they would help them get home unseen. There were rumours of a big bad wolf, but they would rather risk it.

They were all anxious about what was to come, but they did not spot any wolves. Instead, as night approached, they encountered a little lamb.

He was extremely cute. His wool was white as snow, and he said he was the Capricorn's emissary and had a message. He seemed trustworthy, and to prove that he was a heavenly herald, he set fire to a bush. Without any matches. The three goats had never seen such a thing. Then the little lamb continued in his finest voice, "Hear this message: The Seter is set far away and the troll put in between because the goats shall stay in the valley. You are not supposed to go to paradise yet but wait for a calf to come."

Big Billy Goat Gruff replied, "I hear you. But why should we believe you?"

The little lamb continued in his sweetest voice, "It is not part of the plan that you should overcome the troll. Nor have you.

The nasty brute is not only alive but is now more dangerous than before. He will soon be back under the bridge. The Capricorn asks you to stay away. Understand that you are part of a larger plan and that the Seter must wait. The troll lives there to guard the road, and you disturb a greater clockwork by bringing the herd."

Middle Billy Goat Gruff buttered in, "And you want us to wait for how long? There is a blight affecting these mountains that only gets worse. Everything eats at itself and nothing gets better. Even the water is poisoned."

The lamb looked at the three goats. He was obviously not omniscient. "So, you know about the water," he said. "Then you must have talked to the plants or the stoats, but it does not matter. They do not know everything either, and I advise you to stay away. The process is almost complete. Wait for the calf."

He looked up at the stars.

"The Capricorn wants it that way," he said.

"So, you have advised us," replied Big Billy Goat Gruff. "For that I thank you. But I will ask you to leave, because such trust is an unreliable contract. I have met the Capricorn and you are not of the light. You have a distinctly different smell."

As the little lamb looked at him, he suddenly began changing shape. The wool turned dark and soon, in front of them stood a rugged and grey-black goat. He was huge, his horns as old as the mountains. He took a few steps forward. And the closer he got, the darker the night became.

The biggest billy goat met his eyes. He prepared for battle, but the stranger grinned. He watched the crows gather in the sky. "I could easily crush you," he said, setting another tree on fire. "But I am a force aware of my purpose. I do not intervene in that way. I am also part of a plan."

"And what's the plan?" asked the second brother. "Why is it okay to create problems for others, when everyone could be fine?"

The stranger replied, "This is not for goats to know. You are insignificant. You merely live on the edge of a larger universe, and a cycle is about to end. You will have access to the Seter, just wait."

"So everyone's coming to the Seter soon?" asked the little brother, confused.

The stranger smiled. "Yes," he said. Then, after a pause, he added, "Those who want to."

Chills ran down the big brother's spine.

He knew that he had to save the herd at all costs.

He countered, "You say a lot, but you are not all-seeing. You didn't know that we knew about the water, or that we had talked to the stoats. Instead, you reveal that you have poisoned the earth, so why should we listen to you? Why are you intent on destroying us?"

The stranger replied, "It's not about you. As I said, you are insignificant. It's the Water of Life I'm concerned with, and it's only a coincidence that the source is here."

The three goats stared into the abyss that was the stranger's eyes. He clearly had a bigger plan in mind, one that did not bode well for goats, but they could not see the big picture. The reason remained obscure.

The stranger noticed their bewilderment.

He sneered and continued, "But know that I have no ambition to destroy. Actually, I like you, and that's why I want you to wait. The Seter is not for you, not yet. You must wait until the world is ready, and the herd is of no use. Their will is weak. The formerly proud tribe of mountain goats is now like sheep seeking their shepherd's safety, and this would have been the case even without my help."

As he continued, his voice revealed a hatred. "There never was much spirit in them, and I have taken the water to speed up a larger process. A new era is approaching, and they have been sitting on the fence for too long. Now they must show who they are, and everyone will get what they deserve. Just wait for the calf."

The three goats did not know that the wizard had tainted the spirit of the times before destroying the First Spring. The last step was just additional insurance for things to go his way and he felt confident of the stupidity of others. In fact, he had relied upon it thus far. He therefore registered the three goats as no threat to him. He saw how they had lost a lot of fat and knew that the winter would be hard. He also knew what it was like in the valley and he was confident that the goats would stay there till the end. Fear kept them there, and fear had a good hold over them.

But little did he know that the three brothers were not like others. The youngest may have been shaking, but he stepped forward and said, "I don't know much about your game. But I know that there is a Seter so generous that we can all go there. Every other animal knows that too. And they are on their way. That troll is nothing to us."

The stranger suddenly realized that he could not change the will of the goats. He therefore said mockingly to the big brother: "I could have put ten trolls on that bridge but no matter. One is more than enough. There is no chance that you can rouse the herd, and I have never seen anything more stupid than the Capricorn. Do you think the others will see the light?"

He laughed. A wicked laugh. "His prophets have walked the earth for thousands of years. Yet the world remains the same."

He spat on the ground before continuing, "Never have I seen a weaker lineage. Fear reigns from cradle to grave. And you think things will get better?"

He laughed contemptuously. "You can do nothing about the stupidity of the herd. They all eat out of my hand. I've been to your valley. I am in fact coming from there now. Go and see. Things have not improved."

The stranger then transformed into a

crow, and, in a flash, was gone with the murder.

The three brothers felt their hearts racing. They were left with more questions than answers, but the biggest billy goat said, "You did the right thing, brother. I am proud of you. The valley is not far. Let's go home and tell others what we have seen."

Some time passed before the three goats reached the vale. First, they had to climb the rocky walls to the highland plateau. It was a treacherous climb, but there it was—the valley. A cold wind blew through the forests as they moved along, making them shiver. To their surprise, not a soul could be seen in the first village. Nor in the second, or the third. Just a lot of signs everywhere.

They were walking on a forest path and almost home when they met a band of sheep from the Kongsgård.[2] This group came marching towards them and did not seem pleased. The leader stepped forward. "This is the king's guard," he announced. "I am the Sergeant. What are you doing here? Why do you not obey the king's command?"

The three billy goats glanced at each other. They knew the sergeant from school. He had been a lively sheep but was now changed. His eyes were dim, the light in them almost extinguished. He did not even seem to remember them, so the little brother spoke, "Hi Alastair, do you not recognise us? It's us, the three brothers Gruff."

The little billy goat smiled at the sergeant. He was convinced that Alastair was in there somewhere and desperately hoped that their old friend would recognise them. However, the sergeant assumed a grim look and continued, "Announcements have been made everywhere that the mountain air is dangerous. You must have authorisation to be outside."

The three goats looked at each other again. The big brother replied, "Listen, we know nothing about the king's directives. We have had a long journey. We have fought against the troll and been on the Seter. But we have vital news. Can you carry a message for the king?"

There was a discussion amongst the sheep before the sergeant said, "Read the decree!"

He pulled down a poster from a tree and showed it to the three goats. Big Billy Goat Gruff read from it:

"O-R-D-E-R-F-R-O-M-T-H-E-K-I-N-G."

"T-H-O-S-E-W-I-T-H-O-U-T-P-E-R-M-I-S-S-I-O-N-S-H-A-L-L-S-T-A-Y-I-N-S-I-D-E."

"T-A-L-K-I-N-G-A-B-O-U-T-T-H-E-T-R-O-

L-L-A-N-D-S-E-T-E-R-I-S-A-L-S-O-F-O-R-B-I-D-D-E-N."

The three goats glanced at each other yet again, but not for long. The sergeant barked, "Arrest these criminals! It's 20 years for breaching the king's law. You get sixty for breaching three!"

The three goats were instantly surrounded by sheep. The sergeant, pleased, thought of his promotion. "This turned out very fine," he mused. Here, he had captured three triple-criminals, a rare commodity. He would receive infinite rewards for this feat.

"You will be taken to the king's court," he announced. "Attempts to escape will be punishable by death."

Terrified, the little brother sought the warmth and comforting presence of his big brother. A cruel chill was in the air, but it was not coming from the mountains. Nearby, a couple of heads stuck out of windows. Some of these were familiar, but no one said a thing in their defence. Big Billy Goat Gruff assured the others that there would be a solution as soon as they talked to the king. They therefore did not resist when they were cuffed by the flock of sheep.

The king himself lived in a larger city. He rarely visited the remote estate, but the local animals now had their own thing going. Ringer, the old goat at the abbey, had been visited by a distant relative. He had arrived as unnoticed as he departed but, in the meantime, several laws had been made. These laws were designed to protect against looming danger and the royal estate had become an important place. The animals living there liked the idea of defending the valley and soon, a major project connected to this was in progress.

Under the leadership of Ringer and the

monastery, more and more animals had been put in charge of others, and the small valley had seen its first court system. The pigs were eager to become judges, while the sheep and dogs had an inclination for law and order. The cats were totally useless. The cows too—they did not see the point. But the rats, chickens and mice organised the bureaucracy. In this manner, the king's estate stopped producing food and instead, was provided food by animals in the valley.

To sustain this new state of affairs, new laws were made. The horses, bulls, and asses were set to manage these laws, and the Kongsgård was rebuilt. It represented the king's authority, and those in authority now had to have prisons, of course, to punish criminals who dared to break the law.

This is where the three billy goats were taken.

On their way, they saw more signs than animals. Fear was running rampant across the king's land, and the brothers were put in custody.

There they sat for a while. Friends and family visited, but there was nothing anybody could do. Only a few were allowed to visit and when the brothers spoke about the troll, the Seter, and the wizard, only mother did not look away. She believed in her children but could not speak the truth. The more she tried, the more problems she had. And because no one wanted to hear her, good old mom settled for aiding with practical affairs.

The three brothers did not fare much better.

After spending the winter in custody, they were presented at the king's court. There, they got to explain themselves before a judge; however, they never saw the king himself.

At first, the pigs assumed that the three Billy Goats Gruff were lying. Then, when they realised that the goats believed in their own story, they surmised that they had lost their sanity in the Misty Mountains or that the mountain air had become too much. That the three brothers had stood up against trolls and wizards and grazed themselves fat on the heavenly heath—this, the animals could not accept. Instead, it was certain that the air up there had become even more dangerous and that the three bucks had imagined it all.

On these grounds, they felt confident that the mystery had been solved. Only perilous mountain air could explain why someone would openly defy the king's order. To protect against this threat, the animals wrote new laws stating that under no circumstances was contact with the mountain allowed. Mammals were only allowed to leave the house after drinking the antidote to mountain air that Ringer and his group had brewed, although it did not seem to help much.

In the meanwhile, the three goats were told that they would be forgiven if they declared that they had been under the influence of the mountain air when the crime took place.

This was a stroke of luck for the brothers. They could choose between this or 60 years in prison. The latter did not particularly hum of fun. They also thought of their mother, who said that they could not change the world from prison and that it was best to escape the king's clutches.

Still, the three brothers Gruff could not accept this alternative. Such a deception, the big brother stated, was worse than 60 years in prison. He would rather live for the truth than the king's laws. The others agreed, and so they decided to flee. It was simple enough, the big brother said, and devised a plan.

During the winter, more and more animals had become dissatisfied with the new regime. The roedeer were the first to disappear, and friends outside spoke of a life that only got worse. Those who prospered were either in the king's service or simply lucky. Food was scarce. What could be found was not distributed fairly, and more and more people started talking about the Seter—in secret, of course.

No one dared to oppose the authorities openly, for this fear was too great. Despite this, as darkness engulfed the valley, the animals sensed a new fire within. More and more realised that something was wrong, and the big brother thought that they could do some good on the run.

He proposed a heroic struggle of resistance and revolt against the Kongsgård. After this, they would guide as many as possible to the Seter. There, together with those waiting, they would find a way to finally defeat the wizard in the snow.

The brothers were, of course, easy to sway. Despite the prohibition, they sensed the crisp mountain air and spring on its way. They felt the urge to fight for truth and justice. They were ready. One quiet night therefore they snuck out of prison and set course for the highlands.

~ 3 ~

TROLLS AND CREATION

The struggle against the king did not proceed as planned. For six years, the three brothers Gruff operated in the mountains. However, the animals in the valley were hard to convince. For six years, the king's power had grown and more and more had become subjected to the Complex. This was the machine that had been created to guard against danger. What began as a local project in the valley had evolved to unite all the royal estates and grown even larger.

The king himself, to retain power, had to ally with the Complex. And so the kingdom was rapidly integrated. As far as forests stretched, and as far as mountains reached, a system was in place to ensure that animals were either increasingly employed in the king's service or imprisoned. New laws created newer laws, which in turn created yet more laws—and everything was focused on keeping away the treacherous mountain air and talk of trolls and Seter. Such rumours created instability. The king feared that if the brothers' mutinous ideas spread, they would not only result in migration but the Complex losing control as well. More and more animals would prefer the mountain air, and it would be difficult to build an empire.

For these reasons, mere whispers of trolls and Seter were enough for the king to sleep poorly. While he may have had all the fine things that money could buy, his dreams were all terrible. And he did not

know if it was because more and more animals were being thrown in jail, or that
others had recently snuck away at night.
Even his closest adviser, a snake, had disappeared. And the king himself, a lion,
did not feel very proud.

No, the world is not what it could have
been, he thought. But he saw no solution
to the avalanche of problems before him.

Neither did the three Billy Goats Gruff.
For six years, they had tried to create
awareness in the valley. But if things had
gotten worse, fear was still on a rise. Several more prisons had been built, and
those who did not fear the mountain air
were terrified of the Kongsgård. It had
become a stronghold and the pigs had
plenty to do. They had received black
robes for their efforts against offend-
ers—of whom there were many.

Assisted by volunteers and the con-
scripted, the pigs meted out punishment.

Prisons were not only full, but the dungeons at the monastery had become places of horrors. With Ringer in charge of intelligence, suspects were increasingly rounded up. Whispers of opposition rarely travelled far before they were picked up by his spies, and his Ministry of Sincerity had a reputation for forcing confessions.

Thus, a reign of terror was kept in place by a system of reward and punishment. And while public dissatisfaction was high, no real underground movement emerged. Too few had united to overthrow the king, and so the three goats were pondering Plan B.

"Isn't it time to go to the Seter?" asked Middle Billy Goat Gruff. He was in his prime and ready for any challenge that came his way. The big brother was also ready for a change in plans. It had been impossible to rouse the animals to fight against their circumstances. They had tried everything but were no closer to their goal than six years before.

As for the magician on Murk Mountain, no one had seen him. However, the three goats knew that he was there. The water had only gotten worse and the mountains appeared to be sinking in on themselves. Plants and wildlife were scarce, and even the Northwind was polluted.

Big Billy Goat Gruff said, "This is a sad state of affairs. But we do not give up on the herd. The spirit of the valley is broken, but it will return. We shall go to the Seter to find our friends and fight the magician. If we can get rid of him, half our problems will be solved."

Little Billy Goat Gruff nodded. But he did not look forward to the journey.

"Don't you remember," he began, "the wizard said he ruled over trolls? He said he had a troll watching the bridge, but we do not know if he has more. It was bad enough last time. What if it is worse during this trip?"

Their little brother was right. The road to the Seter was not for cowards. "Who knows if we will even arrive at our destination?" said the middle brother. "But we're wasting time. If we leave now, the weather will still be with us. There is still time before the snow and we have a good chance."

Middle Billy Goat Gruff sharpened his horns on rocks. He was ready to follow his big brother and toss the troll down the falls.

Big Billy Goat Gruff himself was not afraid. However, he remembered how hard it had been to fight the troll. He then wondered about what the stoat had said: that the trolls could be a solution rather than a problem. But how? The troll on the bridge had not been interested in talking. There had been little else to do but to fight, and that was what he had done.

He looked at his brothers. "It's weird," he said. "Since the meeting with the troll, I have had dreams where the troll and I become friends. Or more than that, it is as if we become one and the world is turned inside out. It's like visiting the Seter, but even better. A thousand times better, actually."

Little Billy Goat Gruff wanted to see the Seter, but not the troll. He too had grown horns, but they were not large yet. He shook his ears. "It could be the wizard deceiving you," he said. "Maybe he wants to lure us into a trap of ten trolls?"

"Then they will have to deal with these horns," said the middle brother. He dug in his hind hooves, raised his front legs, and then rammed his head into a large stone—it was instantly crushed. He nodded contentedly and said, "I don't think the troll's skull is harder than granite. I think we can manage ten trolls, if that is what it takes."

Soon enough, the three brothers set out on their journey. They travelled further into the highlands and away from the valley. But the closer they got to First Mountain, the more uneasy they felt. The area was in ruins; the land was near dead, and the crows' ominous presence and a hounded wind made the trip worse. The thought of the wizard's watchful eyes prompted the three goats to head towards Goblin Gorge to seek cover. It split further as they moved along, and they followed it quite far.

Things had not gone according to plan last time. But, if they were to stay hidden, this was the way to go. Steep walls towered above them, and the three goats felt safe. This is how they continued for a while. Everything went according to plan, and they were past Grayrise, in the forests west of Ill Valley, as they laid down to sleep. They heard wolves, probably bad, but far away. The three brothers were almost asleep when they heard heavy footsteps.

A large creature was passing by, moving to the south, and they lay completely still. Not far away, loud footsteps sounded; they could smell the troll's stench, and the youngest felt ice cold. Marrow and bone frozen, he wished he would never lay eyes on a troll again.

There were certainly more in the world. Or was this the same wicked creature they had encountered at the bridge? Did this mean that the road to the Seter was clear? The troll had gone in the other direction, so it was possible. He felt encouraged.

However, Middle Billy Goat Gruff was not happy. "Heck," he said. "Had the monstrosity come this way, he would have regretted being born."

He launched into a description of how the troll would have met his end, when the big brother interrupted, "It's okay to fight when you have to," he said, "but it's just stupid to seek trouble."

In the last few years, he had thought a lot about the troll. He remembered the battle of life and death, and how the giant had been severely injured. He continued, "The more we look for problems, the more difficult life becomes. We should be glad that the troll went the other way. This way, no one gets hurt, and we can go to the Seter. We just need to get through these woods, past Bluerise, and we will have grass under our hooves. The Green Moors will be uplifting."

The middle brother was still not happy. He had sharpened his horns and wanted to fight the troll. "Feel these horns," he muttered. The vile troll deserved what he had coming. And because Ogre Abyss was to the south, he wanted to go that way—perhaps he would find the troll there.

It was well-known that trolls lived in hiding. "They hide as much as possible," their father had said. The brothers had not given it much thought back then. But now, the middle brother put two and two together and wanted to head towards the Abyss. There, they would find caves and bridges that had been empty for many years, and he figured that the troll was on his way there.

The Abyss itself was an impenetrable void. It lay between a thousand peaks in the south-west, with chasms so large that First Mountain, Second Mountain, and Third Mountain looked small in comparison. This is where the trolls had lived in the old days, and there were several myths about the place. Echoes of a deep sorrow remained in in the air, and those who went there never returned whole. Post-traumatic stress they called it, just from being there. Travelers had not seen any trolls for generations, but an aura of fear still lingered.

And to this desolate place Middle Billy Goat Gruff vowed to go. "You've clearly lost it," said the little brother. "You have indeed finally gone off the rocks." The little kid had heard of the place. He did not want to go, nor did the big brother. Despite this, he said, "I'll come with you. Not to kill, but to make friends with the troll. Think of what we can accomplish. Together, we can defeat the Kongsgård, the king and the Complex."

The middle brother did not approve. He replied that talk was of little use and that they should get rid of the troll altogether. The little brother was also against it. He was certain that he did not want to see another troll ever again. He wanted to go to the Seter and intended to convince the others. "Trolls are impossible," he noted. "Let's just go to the nearest town. I bet it has seen better days."

The big brother also wanted to see the place, so they went to Firstville. It lay to the east, in the direction the troll had come from. They walked and walked and finally, saw the town. Soon, it became obvious that the troll had stopped by.

The first animal they met was an ox who was very dismayed. He was a general charged to protect the town. They had received communication from Nextville that a troll was heading their way. They had prepared for battle, but the troll had swept them all away. Bitten the heads of many, he had. The general swore that this meant war and that the king would hear about this.

"The monster has to be taken out," he said. "At any cost."

Middle Billy Goat Gruff was extremely angry. It was clear that the troll could not be reasoned with and that they had to find him quickly. Animals' lives were in danger. He also thought about the status his big brother had gained. Many called him "Troll Fighter," and he liked the sound of that. It would be nice, he thought, to take down a troll, and he wanted to go to the Abyss. His brothers suggested a visit to the neighbouring town to find out more.

They ended up going to Nextville. And it was clear that the troll had been cruel here.

The inhabitants were angry, and a donkey reported to them that the troll had come from Wayville. He had flattened the location on purpose and taken a detour to wreck the town hall—in short, he was like most trolls; not one to be reasoned with. The donkey mentioned that a company of sheep had tried to arrest the troll before it destroyed the town. But rather than going with them to the station, it had gone berserk. The result had not been pretty.

The three brothers looked at each other and wondered what to do. The troll had gone mad, that much was certain. Even so, the big brother noted, it was hard to tell whether the sheep or the troll had started the fight. The second brother was firm in his opinions, but the little brother said that they should visit the next town. And so they did.

After a long journey, they reached Wayville. As expected, the town was completely destroyed. Here, too, the troll was said to have come from the east. However, it was not sheep who had received him but a hen. She had smelled him before he arrived and had yelled out to the rooster. The rooster in turn had warned others of the danger, and so the inhabitants had escaped. Nevertheless, the troll had destroyed the aspiring city—town hall and all.

The middle brother had no doubt. Now that they had passed through three devastated towns, he was more convinced than ever that the troll had to be killed. The big brother was also worried, but it was clear that everyone had to rest. They settled in the stable for the night, where a snake came to visit them.

The little brother saw her first. She emerged from the hay and introduced herself.

"I'm a messenger," she hissed, her forked tongue appearing. "You are going the wrong way."

The serpent explained that throughout history, there had been secret societies that used black and white magic. It had been about power and control on the one hand and those who wanted to live in freedom on the other. She said that she was part of the Order of Serpents, a secret society of this kind, and was there to help them.

The youngest buck was not reassured. Goats and snakes were not best friends, and he remembered the wizard as well. "I hear you, but why should we believe you?" he asked.

In reply, the snake mentioned that she had talked to the eagle and knew about the encounter with the stoat and the fox. She explained that the earth was suffering. The snakes knew better than anyone how poisoned the earth was, and their order had become a major part of the resistance. "In several circles we manage the underground," she said. "We work for free will and freedom, and we are many."

Little Billy Goat Gruff was not assured. Free will sounded great. Freedom too. But he knew that the two clashed easily. The animals and the king were a good example. The second brother had the same thoughts.

"It sounds as though you have not chosen a side," he said.

The snake eyed them. There was a moment of silence before she continued, "There are two forces clashing, what you call good and evil or light and darkness. But that was not always the case. There was a time when the universe was light and all one. That was before the world was built. The Creator was alone. He could play with ideas, but it was just him. And because he was bored, he decided to make creation more complete. He began to dream and created individuals with free will. In the realm of thought, which is all that really is, all is still one. However, a veil was created, one that made it difficult to see the bigger picture, and the many souls of Creator were distributed over countless universes, which in turn were part of an even larger one, consisting of seven circles. In the five outer circles, light and darkness played a game of duality, but in the innermost sanctuaries, only light could enter."

"Since the beginning of time," she continued, "this has been the basis of existence. This has been the parameters for expansion and value fulfilment. Out here in the third ring, darkness has ruled for a long time, and the Order of the Serpents has never taken sides."

The snake looked at the middle brother. "It has not been necessary," she said. "Forces greater than light and darkness ensure a balance. At all times, the animals have had the opportunity to choose between good and evil. The fields have been rich, the forests large, the mountains strong, the water fresh, and you have been able to forge your destiny. We have been here to monitor it all, as the Creator directed us to. Throughout time, we have been here and never intervened. But not anymore. The balance is not as before. The First Spring is poisoned, the ground tormented. That is why I'm here. The Capricorn and the Wizard have an agreement. They both whisper in ears and let the world take shape. In choosing between the two, the animals decide whether they will eat or help each other, but there is a bigger plan. That has now been disturbed."

Little Billy Goat Gruff got the chills. He realised that life in the small valley was part of a much larger world. He felt like a tiny ant when he imagined how the world of the goats was part of a larger creation where everyone who lived had their own universe. Even seven mountains were insignificant in comparison. And on top of this, there was a game and a plan, that only a few knew about.

He shuddered. Old Hermit had mentioned a game behind a bigger game, but the kid had been none the wiser. What had brought him here? What had made wizards and secret orders interested in three goats?

He had never heard of such a thing. But the stoat had said that the trolls were the saddest of all creatures and that no one had suffered as much as they had. He found it difficult to imagine. Trolls were the absolute worst and it was hard to feel sorry for them. He asked the snake, "Are the trolls part of this plan?"

"Yes and no," she replied. "Yes, because they are here and because they are needed, no because they have suffered for too long."

"The trolls were created before goats or other animals. They were here first and were forced to build the world—not by the Capricorn and the forces of light but by the Opponent. He who never gives gratitude. He who never forgives. And he who always hates. He was the one who created the Pillars of the world, and the trolls built the rest. Since then, trolls have been tied to this creation. They are the ones who nurture the Ground of Being. This is the foundation of creation in five circles, and in their heart is said to lie a key. The wise argue about what this key could be. Many a sorcerer has opened their heart to find out, but no one has found what they were looking for. Instead, they have opened a dark chapter, as the hearts of trolls also carry the despair of the world."

The smallest goat shrugged. "You remind me of the stoat," he said. "He was talking about trolls and a plan."

The snake raised her head.

"Yes, and the Opponent has not kept to the agreement. The agreement was that life would develop in freedom. That the animals would eat each other until they learned to cooperate. But the Water of

Life is poisoned. The balance is broken. And fear prevails. It does not look like the bridge will open."

"The bridge?" asked Big Billy Goat Gruff.

The snake looked at him and replied, "At the end of each era, a window opens. The animals can travel using this and many come to the Seter. This has been the case for a long time, but now the Ground of Being is in jeopardy. The trolls have suffered for too long. They can no longer stand it and they need help. That's why I'm here."

There was another moment of silence before she continued, "The agreement was that the trolls would guard the bridge and be of use. But a long time ago, their will was broken by the Opponent. He told the trolls that he had made them and that they had a fault. He said that one day, they would be free, but only if they obeyed. He has ruled them with fear ever since, and he betrays them every time."

"Every time?" queried the second brother.

"Yes, countless promises have been broken. It's an ugly story."

Big Billy Goat Gruff felt great unease.

"But what about the Capricorn?" he asked. "Why will he not intervene? It does not seem right at all!"

The snake looked at him. "No," she said. "But there is more we do not understand. And I'm asking you not to kill the troll. But find him. Go to Skyrise."

She looked at the middle buck. "I know your horns are hard and your will is strong. But remember that this is the first time our order has intervened. Since the dawn of time, we have let the river flow. Now we ask it to slow."

The youngest still longed for the Seter. "Isn't it better if we go there?" he asked.

The snake knew about the place. She had been there before. "It's a dream," she said. It has been put there for the plan to work, but it is not real. You found it because you tried more than others, but it is not just about following the path."

The three goats looked at each other in confusion.

What were they to believe?

The snake gazed at Second Billy Goat Gruff. "Remember this," she said. "The wise know that the Creator is dreaming and that one day, he will wake up. They just do not know how. The trolls can be a key."

The middle brother thought hard. Trolls had been fought many times, but things had only gotten worse. It was difficult to see any solution. He did not believe that they could be pacified.

The snake perceived his doubt. However, she had delivered her message. She weaved towards the hay before turning and repeating, "Remember, the Creator is dreaming."

She looked at the three goats, smiled, and added, "He can play with ideas, but it's still just him."

The snake slithered away in the hay as swiftly as she had come.

The three brothers looked at each other. They did not know if the wizard was behind all this. But the snake wanted them to go to Skyrise, the world's highest mountain. Although it was not very far away—it was closer than the Seter—it was still a peak in the Misty Mountains, which was not encouraging.

"I think it was the wizard in one of his many forms," said Middle Billy Goat Gruff. He believed it was a ruse, that the troll was in the Abyss, and that they should go there.

Big brother was sceptical. He had not noticed the same odour from the snake that he had before with the wizard. He replied, "The snake seemed truthful enough. I think we should go to Skyrise and talk to the troll. Let's head south."

The little brother protested, "I thought middle brother was a nut. But you have lost it for sure! There's no way I'm going there. You said it yourself, no one comes back."

"Some must be the first," said Big Billy Goat Gruff. "Middle brother wants to find trolls, and so do I. Something tells me that the snake was right and that we must go there. Without the troll, we do not stand a chance, and the Seter is not what it appears to be. For all we know, it was a dream. Let's find the Misty Mountains."

The other brothers were not keen on this plan. Not at all. However, big brother was adamant, and soon, they were heading south.

They continued on for a long time before finally arriving at the Misty Mountains. These were a long belt of crags to the south, and no one knew what lay on the other side. The goats only knew that on clear days, a peak could be seen above the fog—and this was Skyrise.

Little Billy Goat Gruff gazed into the distance. There, somewhere deep in the haze, a troll awaited them. He did not know what would be worse: the troll or the trek. He also felt extremely anxious. The task seemed impossible. He was determined to help his brothers but was certain of death—he only hoped that it would be quick and painless.

The others also dreaded the road ahead. They all thought of their family and friends back home. Would they ever see them again?

The fog grew thicker and thicker, and it became more difficult to see. However, the landscape was delightful. It took their mind off friends and family and became more and more captivating as they pushed ahead.

That is how they moved for a long time. After a while, the youngest felt that he did not miss his mother so much. The valley, the Seter, and the troll had also faded in importance. It all seemed quite insignificant in comparison to the landscape. The stony terrain only became more interesting the more they climbed. Strangely enough, it was as if the scenery and their meditations had become one. The rock and the fog spoke not only to them but through them as well. They each heard whispers of sweet dreams. Suddenly, the big brother understood what was happening.

"This place is dangerous," he said. "The mist is taking control. I have no idea where we are going."

Big Billy Goat Gruff was right. They had been wandering a long time. They did not know for how long and they had been made blind to their goal. The youngest and middle brother did not even remember meeting any troll, but their big brother soldiered onwards.

"We have to get out of the fog," he said. "Nothing has been making sense for days now, and I must make every effort to break out of this. I think we have kept to a certain direction, but I'm not sure."

The three goats looked at each other. The younger brothers did not recognise their big brother, nor each other. The bond of family, however, was strong and held them together. They had been walking like this for a long time, but big brother could hardly think. His mind was dull, his memory full of holes.

He was soon ready to give up. Where were they? What were they doing? Nothing made sense anymore. He looked around. All he could see was fog and more fog. His brothers were not there anymore. He tried but could not remember the last time he had seen them. A memory of them not understanding anything and him being unable to help them, briefly flashed across his mind. But he could not remember when or where. His mind was almost blank. And eventually, the mist captured all his attention. It promised rest, and he soon fell asleep.

. . .

Big Billy Goat Gruff had no idea how long he had slept. But now he felt a breeze. A fresh new wind came from west, and he took a deep breath.

The wind was refreshing, and some of his memories returned. The big billy goat remembered who he was and opened his eyes.

He saw a roedeer in front of him. He had not seen them for years, but this was still no ordinary sight. It was as if the wind was coming from the stag himself. He was of light and had a spring in his step that made the grass grow thick and green. The wind was healing all life, and the stag moved gracefully on nimble legs.

The big brother took another breath. It was the best air he had ever known. It drove the fog away, turned the grey landscape to green, and down the mountain, he spotted his brothers. They were climbing over a mount and appeared like their old selves again. The fresh air had not only found them in time but had kept the fog away as well.

The three goats were overjoyed to see each other, and the stranger came towards them.

"Hi," said the roedeer. He glowed. The grass around him got greener. Flowers sprang up around his feet, and life flourished. It was quite a sight.

He looked at them. "You have met messengers before," he said. "But none like me."

They waited for the stag to continue, but he looked up at the precipices above them and ran on. The green grass on the ground disappeared with him. So did the fresh air.

The three goats looked down and saw that the mist was rising once again.

They realised that they had to act fast. They climbed up the mountain, away from the mist. So they continued for a while, until the fog no longer threatened to catch up to them. It remained below, waiting.

Once they had ascertained that they were safe, they looked around. To their surprise, they saw that they had found Skyrise.

The great mountain stretched upwards as far as the eye could see. However, there was no life to be seen, only stone. Surrounded by this sight, they continued to climb for many days.

Sometimes, the big brother imagined that he could smell the same fresh air that he had woken up to. It was in these areas that the goats also found food. It was not much, but enough to keep them going. Grass and water appeared when all hope seemed lost.

This is how time passed. The three brothers climbed and climbed, and finally, one dawn, they saw the summit.

Little Billy Goat Gruff was walking behind the others. They had been climbing all night and the sharp walls had kept them close to certain death. Yet, it was as if they were being carried by a force. As he approached the summit, the force returned. Was there a sense of expectation in the air? He felt a new sensation—it whispered to him. It got stronger. The little brother looked up. There was the troll.

A wind was blowing, but it was coming from within. It was the same wind that he had felt down the mountain, and which had awakened him from the overpowering slumber. He still recalled it invigorating all life. It strengthened him.

He looked at the others. They had stopped dead. They, too, had seen the troll.

"Up there is the troll," said the little billy goat. "Are you ready?"

Middle Billy Goat Gruff turned. He felt his legs tremble as fear permeated him. It was easy to strike a rock. But this was something else entirely. Something older. Something he did not understand. He smelled its stench and did not like it. A chill went through him. He stood motionless, feeling an overwhelming sense of anxiety. Something monumental was about to unfold. And he was not ready for it.

The big brother also did not know what to do. He did not see the point in talking to the troll. He smelled the stench himself—of blood and desolation. Of sin and shame. He felt contempt for this monster. He felt the strong urge to gore it once and for all. Properly this time.

The little brother observed this.

"But," he asked, "aren't we supposed to talk to it?"

Big brother was repulsed by the suggestion. He thought about all the evil and despicable acts perpetrated by this monster. Over time, it had probably amounted to a lot.

"I don't think so," he said. "Nobody has done it before, and I don't know what to say."

"Better to be prepared for the worst," he continued. "I suggest that middle brother and I go up, while you wait here."

The youngest goat saw the sense in this. But he realised that fear was in charge and that there would be a major conflict at the summit.

"No," he replied. "You wait here, while I talk to the troll. If there is one thing the troll is afraid of, it's your horns. And you would not be of much use either, middle brother. You are full of fear and anger, whereas I feel calm. I have always been scared, but no more. Let me face the troll."

The little goat did not wait for an answer. He walked up to his brothers, who stepped aside to let him pass. They were surprised, but little brother gave them hope. They had never seen such courage. They nodded approvingly, bowed, and Little Billy Goat Gruff walked towards the troll.

He climbed a short distance to reach the top. Dawn was breaking and the troll was in sight. It sat there looking at the dying night sky.

As the little brother moved closer, the troll turned. It looked down at him, but the little goat did not feel small. He felt not only a new wind within him, but a new fire as well. It burned brightly. It was as if his chest was filled with light. As if each of his cells was lit. He walked completely up to the troll.

"What are you doing here?" asked the little billy goat.

The troll had seen goats before, but not one like this. In fact, through countless of years the troll had never felt such energy. It was a key. It opened a lock.

The troll exhaled. A teardrop was gathering in his eye—and somewhere deep inside, and around him, a new heart began to beat.

The little billy goat had no idea what he had done. However, there is no heart as big as that of a troll, and the universe could feel the change in its beat reverberating all the way to the Ground of Being.

A shiver went through the troll, and he said, "I am here because I'm tired. Across time, trolls have borne all the blame. Ingratitude is all we have received. I could bear it no more. Our Maker is fear himself. He demanded everything but gave nothing but pain in return. It was terror and slavery from dusk till dawn. We had to obey the will of He who never forgives. He who always hates. He who wants to enthral.

It was he who told me to guard the bridge. I have been watching it for longer than time itself. And I could do it no more. I decided to leave. I came here, where no one else lives. Here, it is just me and the stars, and here, silence has found me. Through this calm, I have found comfort. I have just not seen hope."

As he spoke, the other goats climbed up the hillside, ready for a confrontation.

The troll turned towards them. The situation became tense, and the middle brother could feel an adrenaline rush.

The troll was ugly, but not very frightening. He saw something recognisable in its eyes, although he did not know what—he quickly brushed this thought aside. Instead, he felt his confidence rising at the possibility of a quick victory.

The second brother asked the troll, "Why did you bother us on the bridge? We were on our way to the Seter, what was wrong with that?"

"Uhm, err," mumbled the troll.

"I'm really sorry. You met me on a bad day. For aeons, I had only known darkness. I was alone—always had been—and was asleep. Until I was awakened by the crows."

The troll continued, "I thought it was Maker testing me. I had not seen travellers for over 300 years, and when your brother appeared, I thought it was him. I had to be a powerful presence. You could not pass. It would have been severe punishment, lots of suffering and even more grief. I did not want that. I therefore waited to take you all at once. I thought Maker would be proud. He took the Maid. We trolls live long, but not well without. And Maker took her. I hoped Maker would give back the Maid."

"Did you get her back?" asked the smallest goat.

"No," responded the troll. "Only a bigger debt and more misery."

Big Billy Goat Gruff asked, "But why did you not run away or try to liberate the Maid?"

The troll replied, "No one knows where she is. In fact, I have never seen her, or any other Maid. Nor have any other troll. But we know that they must exist somewhere; they are our other half, and we long to be complete."

Little Billy Goat Gruff saw the longing in his eyes. "But why do you say that Maker has taken her?" he asked.

The troll answered, "This is what Maker told me and this is what he tells every troll. He says that he shall keep every Maid until our debt is paid."

"And when will it be paid?" asked the big brother. "What is your sin and when will you be free?"

"I have no idea," responded the troll. "Several cycles have passed since any troll dared to ask Maker. He burns and wounds us if we do. I finally ran away. I escaped at night, in search of the mountain."

"But why did you destroy the three towns?" asked the middle brother.

"I'm also sorry about that," replied the troll.

"As I said, I prefer to travel at night. No one saw me, except a hen. She screamed and the whole town ran. I was already sad. At this point, depression overwhelmed me. This was my first contact with animals in many years, but it did not go as planned. After this setback, I went berserk, and the same happened in the other towns."

The troll sighted deeply. He looked at his swollen fist. "I have a problem with anger," he said. "It overwhelms me. I have been alone for too long and was hoping for a new start."

He looked down in shame and continued, "We trolls are not very wise. But our Firstborn believed that we would be the beginning of something new. That we should endure suffering, but bear it boldly, for something greater to happen. And ever since, trolls have been waiting for that day when something magical will happen. I have had dreams about this.

About something that does not hurt. They're the only nice dreams I've ever had. And I got so angry that I flattened the three towns. From there, this was the only way. Away from everyone."

The three goats looked at each other.

The middle brother looked at the troll. He did not want to fight him anymore. He realised that the troll was not that bad.

"Are you going to live here forever?" he asked.

The troll had not thought that far ahead. "I do not know," he replied. "With the stars, one finds perspective, but only in meeting with others do we discover ourselves."

The troll looked up at the sky. He then looked at the three brothers and said, "I now know that isolation is an illusion. That all life is connected in thought no matter what. And that fear and love rule everything. It was fear of not being good enough that made me live in the dark. It was a dread on so many levels that made me fight with others, and it was the sum of this fear that brought me here."

The troll paused, contemplated his situation, and continued, "I would have liked to go back. However, once you have a bad reputation, others are quick to judge. I noticed this many cycles ago and things have not changed. The animals hate me. I see no point in returning."

"But I do not hate you," said Middle Billy Goat Gruff. "I thought I had found a worthy enemy, one I could vanquish. But I understand that I was wrong."

Big Billy Goat Gruff was pleased that his brother had found forgiveness. He butted in, "It turns out that the ox, the ass, and the other villagers knew nothing about the troll. Instead, they showed us what we should have known all along: that when someone talks about others, they are mostly talking about themselves. The animals had no idea that it was love that moved the troll towards the town. Why things went sour, therefore, had more to do with the troll's appearance than his intention. And the moral of the story is that we have to look past facades. Only then can we overcome our fears."

He looked at his brothers and added, "What we should do, is bring the troll with us. Once the other animals understand that we are friends, they will have to reconsider their prejudices."

The others thought this was wise. "But would you join us?" asked the youngest goat.

The troll thought about it, and replied: "Yes, more than anything. If others can look past my hideousness, the beauty in me can live. And who knows, maybe together we can create a better world."

"You are saying something wise," answered big brother. "But be warned, things are not going well. The king has enslaved the land and the Opponent has destroyed the Water of Life. We must do something. Do you want to help us save the world?"

The answer was obvious. A new wind was blowing. The force that had saved them from the fog and brought them to the pinnacle of the world was urging them on. They all knew it. The troll too. They were connected. A force stronger than nature dwelled in them. It had placed them there for a reason, and it was near completion.

All around them, the earth was moving. Grass and flowers rose from the ground, and beetles and other creatures filled the air. The wind was fresh, clean, and gentle.

Heaven had never been so near. Even up there, on the highest mountain, dragonflies and butterflies appeared. Not only that, but a new Consciousness of the World emerged, more brilliant, more wholesome than before.

The three brothers thought about the Great Game—and the even bigger game behind it. Was this the time long foretold when the lion and the lamb were to live together? Was this the road to the Seter? Or was it something else? Did the rest of the world have to wait for the awakening? No matter, it was a miracle in unfolding. They could see it all around. The Creator was moving. He was in everything.

Big Billy Goat Gruff wondered aloud, "We have heard that there is a bigger game, one the Opponent does not know about. He does not know about it because we are in the Creator's dream, and he is asleep.

But what will happen when he wakes up?"

The big brother gazed towards the horizon.

The others were quiet.

He continued, "I ask because there is a king and a wizard out there. But we have heard that darkness is part of Creator's dream. If this is true, what happens to evil if light is all that is? If darkness is the light that has forgotten itself, will it disappear and will everyone know their true selves?"

Still, no one said a thing.

"It's hard to tell," he sighed. "The world has never seen such an awakening. Countless ages have passed and the cycles have been the same. Light and darkness have fought for souls, but the Creator is asleep. No single soul can wake him. We are trapped in his dream until enough wake up to Creator within. I wonder how many are left? How many do we have to be to end the dream?"

They looked at each other.

The troll suddenly burst out laughing. It was his first laugh in his long life.

For the first time, he could imagine a different creator than the Maker. A destiny other than that of a slave and scapegoat. He envisioned a creator who was good. Who would give him everything, and who would never leave his side. For he also saw how everything had led to this. All the pain had a purpose: it was to remind him of something. To help him see a greater Whole—and he saw it. First in the stars, and now everywhere.

He spoke, "Maker said he knew everything about everyone in the five circles. But he did not know about this. A Greater

Hand is touching the surface. This has not happened before. I think the true Creator is about to awaken."

The three Brothers Gruff and the troll looked to the west. They felt the Hand move—a new consciousness was being established. The Veil was torn and they were ready. They had a kingdom to defeat. A herd to help. They leapt down the mountain side—one with the wind. It was not just a new day, but a new world on the rise.

Notes

1. ^ The traditional Seter (from Norwegian Seter or Swedish säter) is a summer pasture, especially one in the mountains of Scandinavia, to which farmers used to take livestock as part of transhumance. Its connotations are utopian and the Seter is an embedded part of Scandinavian folklore.

2. ^ The Kongsgård (Swedish: Kungsgård) is a residence, estate, or farmland that belonged to the Scandinavian monarchs or royal families. During the Viking Age and early Middle Ages, the nations of Scandinavia were organised as frail political unions. To remain in control, kings would frequently travel the land. The Kongsgård would then function as temporary residencies for the kings and gradually developed into larger main estates and fortresses.

 Mikalsen is the author of six books which are changing the world, one at a time. His authorship covers a large area, ranging from cosmology, mysticism, self-help, and consciousness research to power politics, human rights law, drug policy, constitutional interpretation, and social engineering. He is the founder of the Alliance for Rights-Oriented Drug Policies (AROD), an organization which addresses drug policy reform from a perspective of human rights, and a nominee of two prestigious human rights awards (Vaclav Havel and Martin Ennals).

A platform for his work is Life Liberty Productions, a publishing house and consulting agency dedicated to the Spirit of Freedom. At its store lifeliberty-books.com, you will find books that are embraced by professionals and have the potential to bring humanity one step further.